Magical World

Snow White is a princess, but she must work as a servant for her evil stepmother. At the wishing well, Snow White makes a wish for true love. One day, she runs away to the forest and makes friends with the Seven Dwarfs. Soon she meets a prince, and her wish comes true.

Ariel has a beautiful voice. 🎵 She loves to sing and dance with her best friend, Flounder. Someday, this Little Mermaid hopes to dance like humans do. She dreams of being part of the world above the sea.

Cinderella peers out the window of her carriage. The moon shines over the palace.

Cinderella sees the clock tower and remembers the Fairy Godmother's warning. She must leave the Prince's royal ball before the clock strikes midnight.

To disguise herself as a man, Mulan cuts her hair. ⬭ She reports to the Imperial Army to take her father's place, for he is ill. Mulan proves herself by climbing a tall pole to retrieve an arrow. After training, the army sets off on horses. ⬭ The soldiers must stop the Hun invaders. ⬭

One day, the Beast decides to surprise Belle with a library full of books. "It's wonderful!" exclaims Belle. The Beast is very happy and so are his enchanted servants. The servants are sure that the Beast and Belle will fall in love.

Princess Jasmine longs to explore the world outside the palace.  One day, a prince named Ali flies to Jasmine's balcony on the Magic Carpet.  As Prince Ali, Aladdin invites the princess to go for a ride. Together, they fly away. "It's all so magical," says Princess Jasmine.

Take a Magic Carpet Ride!

North America

Europe

Asia

Africa

South America

Australia

Antarctica

Captain John Smith and a group of settlers sail from England to a new land. Smith meets Pocahontas, the daughter of a chief. Pocahontas shows Smith the beauty of the land and the spirit of life all around. She says, "We are connected to the river, the creatures, the forest."

At last, Princess Aurora is with her true love.  The three good fairies are filled with joy as they watch Princess Aurora dance with Prince Phillip.

"Oh, I just love happy endings!" Fauna says. The princess will have the wedding of her dreams.